P9-DCI-591

Washington
≋County
Sept 2017
WASHINGTON COUNTY LIBRARY
8595 Central Park Place • Woodbury, MN 55125

Also by Patricia MacLachlan

Edward's Eyes
Fly Away
The True Gift
Waiting for the Magic
White Fur Flying

just dance

Patricia MacLachlan

Margaret K. McElderry Books
New York   London   Toronto   Sydney   New Delhi

MARGARET K. McELDERRY BOOKS

An imprint of Simon & Schuster Children's Publishing Division

1230 Avenue of the Americas, New York, New York 10020

This book is a work of fiction. Any references to historical events, real people, or real places are used fictitiously. Other names, characters, places, and events are products of the author's imagination, and any resemblance to actual events or places or persons, living or dead, is entirely coincidental.

Text copyright © 2017 by Patricia MacLachlan

Jacket illustration copyright © 2017 by Amy June Bates

All rights reserved, including the right of reproduction in whole or in part in any form.

MARGARET K. McELDERRY BOOKS is a trademark of Simon & Schuster, Inc.

For information about special discounts for bulk purchases, please contact Simon & Schuster Special Sales at 1-866-506-1949 or business@simonandschuster.com.

The Simon & Schuster Speakers Bureau can bring authors to your live event. For more information or to book an event, contact the Simon & Schuster Speakers Bureau at 1-866-248-3049 or visit our website at www.simonspeakers.com.

Book design by Debra Sfetsios-Conover

The text for this book was set in ITC New Baskerville.

Manufactured in the United States of America

0817 FFG

First Edition

10 9 8 7 6 5 4 3 2 1

Library of Congress Cataloging-in-Publication Data

Names: MacLachlan, Patricia, author.

Title: Just dance / Patricia MacLachlan.

Description: First edition. | New York : Margaret K. McElderry Books, [2017] | Summary: On a farm in the middle of the prairie, ten-year-old Sylvie struggles to understand why her mother gave up singing on stage while she sets off on an adventure of her own as the town reporter.

Identifiers: LCCN 2016040532 | ISBN 9781481472524 (hardcover) | ISBN 9781481472548 (eBook)

Subjects: | CYAC: Families—Fiction. | Country life—Fiction. | Singers—Fiction. | Reporters and reporting—Fiction.

Classification: LCC PZ7.M2225 Ju 2017 | DDC [Fic]—dc23

LC record available at https://lccn.loc.gov/2016040532

This is John's book—
with thanks to Jack Barry, who began it
—P. M.

My gratitude to Sylvia Lanka, who sings

Life is simple, but we insist on
making it complicated.

—*Confucius*

Life is the dancer
and you are the dance.

—*Eckhart Tolle*

Just Dance

I grew up on a farm, and I'm ten, so I don't
know much about love. I know about cattle,
chickens, two goats, sheep, and how to ride
a horse.

But I know love when I see it.

My mother was a professional soprano
until she met my father. She studied in Europe
and sang opera and performed concerts and
wore big silk dresses until she came back
to America and walked into a small diner in
Wyoming. My father saw her. He stood up and
walked over.

He held out his hand.

And they danced.

There was country music playing. My mother knew nothing about country music. She'd never heard of Johnny Cash or Tammy Wynette or "Stand by Your Man" or "Ring of Fire."

My mother danced with him. Later he would teach her the Texas Two-Step.

My father is a cowboy and my mother a classical soprano. They might seem far apart in life.

But my mother loved my father right away.

"When I looked into his eyes I felt like I was looking into the eyes of a very wise horse," she said.

My mother is better at singing than at words.

"Your mother was more beautiful than evening light," says my father.

My father is very good with words. He carries books of poetry and short stories in his saddlebag.

So here is a rule.

If you want to find the love of your life, go to the Hideaway Café in Cheyenne, Wyoming. When a tall cowboy with a ponytail comes up to you and takes your hand, you don't have to speak. It's better not to speak, actually.

Just dance.

By Sylvie Bloom
Grade 4

• 1 •

Sweet Songs and Stinkbugs

My father, my younger brother Nate, and I sat on the hallway floor outside the one bathroom in our house. You might think we were waiting to use the bathroom, but that was not so.

We were listening to my mother sing. She likes to sing in the bathroom when she takes a shower. My father tiled the entire room, in fact. The tiles bounce her voice around so she can hear herself.

In the attic I found large posters of my mother, all dressed up in taffeta or silk, singing in great halls, fancy chandeliers above her. Her name, Melinda May, was written in large, important letters. Now my father calls her Min and she sings to the animals and in the tiled bathroom of our farmhouse.

When she sings in the shower we come to hear her. Nate hears my whistle and hurries in from the barn. My father comes in from the fields. Once he left his horse Jack by the back door and we later found Jack in the kitchen.

We heard the slap of the screen door, and Bett, our herding dog, came down the hallway to lie down next to my father.

"The herd is safe. Bett has come to be with

her pack and listen," said my father softly.

My father set his cowboy hat on the floor next to him, his head leaning against the wall. His eyes were closed.

My mother's voice sounded lovely and clean, like newly washed glass.

"*Un bel dì*," my father said softly.

"'A fine day.'"

My mother may not know all things about Johnny Cash, but my father has studied Puccini, who wrote the song my mother sings. My father knows all of my mother's songs and who wrote them—Puccini, Bizet, Mozart, and Donizetti.

My brother, Nate, pointed to a stinkbug crawling down the wall.

There is something about my eight-year-old brother, Nate—a sort of sly sweetness when he points out the strangely homely with the beautiful.

"Lovely," whispered Nate with a grin.

My father—good with words, remember—said Nate understands the connection of opposites: the sleek, shapely body of the bug and his bad smell.

"Summer vacation soon," said Nate.

I turned my head to look at Nate. "Do you ever want something exciting to do away from the farm in the summer? To see amazing things?"

Nate shook his head. "I'm happy here," he whispered. "It's amazing here. And exciting."

"I need something new," I said. "Something more interesting than cows and goats and chickens."

"Chickens are very, very interesting,"

said Nate. "Millie even likes to sit on my lap. Buddy plays tag with me."

"I need something different," I said.

"It will happen," said Nate. "It will."

I smiled because Nate sometimes sounds like a wise old man.

My mother finished her aria on a high, long note. She turned off the shower.

My father quickly got up. He didn't want my mother to be shy about us listening when she sang in the shower. Nate hurried off. Bett trotted after them.

All that was left behind was my father's handkerchief. And the stinkbug crawling back up the wall again, direction changed.

My mother came out of the shower and bent down to pick up the handkerchief.

She knew.

My mother knew everything.

Almost everything.

I wondered why she's happy singing in the shower instead of wearing a big silk dress and singing for a huge audience, who, when she is finished, leap to their feet and applaud. And someone gives her a huge bunch of flowers onstage as the velvet curtain falls.

Today I found a letter left open on the kitchen table for me to read. It was from James Grayson, a famous tenor, to my mother.

Melinda—

I will be singing a concert close to you. Please come. Maybe we can sing together again! I'll send you tickets.

James

I turned the letter over as if hiding it from myself. I remembered a large, fancy poster with a picture of my mother and James, looking happy and famous. How could she leave that behind to live on a farm in the middle of the prairie?

It is hard to believe that loving my father is enough.

It is hard to believe that Nate and I are enough.

• 2 •

A Perfect Day

I didn't like the last day of fourth grade. I loved the fourth grade, mostly because I love my teacher, Mrs. Ludolf. Mrs. Ludolf loves me, too, which helps.

I will miss her when I go to fifth grade.

She knows I can write. She wrote back to me on my stories. She asked questions.

"Really??" she writes with disbelief.

"LOVE this!"

"Ugh."

"I don't understand this sentence. What do you really mean?"

She is always right.

"Spelling is more important than you think," she once told the class. She sighed.

I knew she was thinking about her husband, Sheriff Ludolf, who can't spell. He writes Ludolf's Log in the newspaper every day, all about town events.

"He's a very smart man who learned English when he was older," she said. "But he can't spell."

We know that by reading the log.

Teddy Dunn's goats ran wildlee around town. Mrs. Pheasant fell down in her nightgown.

Madd cat will not let Maude Willie in her house. Jake Willie couldn't stop laffing and had to be taken to the hospital.

Just this week he wrote:

Billy Reem's bulls got out and ran down the road. We were afraid they might become violet.

Violet?

I knew the sheriff meant "violent."

I like his logs because they are puzzles waiting to be solved. I told Mrs. Ludolf this.

She stared at me for a long time.

"I hope you keep writing all summer while school is out," she said.

"I don't know if I can," I said. "I work better

with assignments. I like to see the things I'll write about."

Sometimes Mrs. Ludolf says to write about:

light
why I'm crying
what a shelter dog wishes for
your favorite time of day or night
what your cat does at night while you sleep

And the morning after we listened to my mother sing "*Un bel dì*" in the shower—

After we watched her sing to the cows in the meadow and they ran in to be milked—

After she tried, as always, to charm the goats by singing and they bleated her away—

There was a knock at our door.

It was Mrs. Ludolf with Sheriff Ludolf.

"Come in, Rudolph. Come in, Ella," said my father.

I didn't know Sheriff Ludolf's name was Rudolph Ludolf. It made me smile.

And I never knew Mrs. Ludolf was Ella. I guess most of us in fourth grade thought of her first name as "Mrs."

They came in and sat down at the kitchen table. My mother was out singing a lullaby to the pigs. We could hear her sweet voice through the door. Her singing always caused the pigs to stop and stare, frozen in place, so she could shovel out their pens.

"'*Caro nome.*' *Rigoletto*," said my father. "It means 'Sweet name.'"

Sheriff Ludolf gestured to the page of the newspaper. "What mistake did I make today?" he asked.

"Only a small one," I told him kindly, because I could see he was worried. "You wrote 'turkies' with an 'i-e-s' instead of 'turkeys' with an 'e-y-s.' Not too bad."

Sheriff Ludolf smiled at me.

"We came to give Sylvie two pieces of news," said Mrs. Ludolf. "Good news, I hope."

"For me?" I said.

Nate sat down at the table.

Mrs. Ludolf nodded.

"I'll tell her, Ella," said Sheriff Ludolf. "I may not be able to spell, but I can talk. My wife has a summer assignment for you."

"She does? What?"

"Me," said Sheriff Ludolf.

He took a piece of paper out of his pocket. "This is a contract. I'd like to hire you to write Ludolf's Log this summer."

"Your assignment," said Mrs. Ludolf happily.

I read the contract.

"You're going to pay me? For writing?!"

"Yes. You'll cover the town, like a reporter. You can ride your horse sometimes. Or ride with me. Maybe once or twice with my deputy, Lula. We'll give you a cell phone so we can report in events when we see them."

My own cell phone.

"I'd like to ride with her the first day," said my father. "We don't get to ride horses together very often."

Suddenly I felt like crying.

My father put his large hand over mine. He knew I was a little afraid. He knew.

"That's just fine, Jack," said Sheriff Ludolf. "You know the town roads."

"And fields and rivers," said Mrs. Ludolf.

She knew I was nervous.

The sheriff handed me a pen from his pocket.

"Do you agree?" he asked.

"I agree!"

I signed my name.

"You'll see amazing things, Sylvie," said Nate. "Just like I said."

"Thank you, Sylvie," said the sheriff. "Ella says you are a great writer. And you can write the log any way you want. And people will stop laughing at me. They call my log 'Ludolf's Looney Log.'"

"Could I write poetry?" I asked.

"You can do whatever you want. Do it your way. Maybe we can call it 'Sylvie's Summer Log.' All righty then!"

Mrs. Ludolf smiled. The sheriff was known for his "well, all righty then!" comment.

The sheriff stood up and he and Mrs. Ludolf walked to the door.

Suddenly Mrs. Ludolf turned. "Do you want to hear the second piece of good news?"

I nodded.

"I'll be your teacher in fifth grade! I get to follow my favorite students."

"Yay!"

I thought I'd said it to myself, but I'd said it out loud.

"Yay!" echoed Mrs. Ludolf.

"I hope I can do this," I said.

"You can," said Mrs. Ludolf. "Remember what you wrote in class. Just dance."

When they opened the door, I had a

summer job as a writer. I had my own cell phone. I had my favorite teacher next year.

And my mother was singing music from *La Traviata* for our small herd of sheep to their loud baas back at her.

A perfect day.

"A perfect day," I repeated to my mother when she came up to say good night.

"I know!" she said. "Perfect like mine. I get to sing every day. You'll get to write every day."

She had a page in her hand with a man's picture.

I reached out for it. "What is this?"

"James Grayson! He sent it to us so we could go hear him."

"I saw a poster of you singing with him. I

saw it in the attic. You were both dressed up."

My mother laughed. "We did dress up in those days!"

She kissed me and went off to her shower.

My mother is wrong. It's not the same at all. She could sing onstage with James Grayson if it weren't for us.

And James was coming.

She could have fame. She could have excitement. I'd write about the town—the cows and horses and sheep that run loose. No surprises. No excitement.

The shower went on. And I knew Nate and my father, gone to bed early, would listen from their beds.

I will hear her too. I don't understand my mother. But I will listen to her song from my bed—"*Casta diva*." Slow and sad, my

mother's favorite evening shower aria.

And the James she sang with is coming.

Will she want to sing onstage, away from us?

I listen.

And then I sleep.

• 3 •

Jack 'n' Jack

Early, before my mother and Nate were out of bed, my father and I saddled up our horses in the morning dark. I rode my Molly with the white blaze. My father's horse was named Jack, like my father. Sometimes the people in the town would joke "here comes Jack 'n' Jack," as if together they made one name.

Jack 'n' Jack.

"That was his name when I bought him," my father once explained. "The only name he'd answer to."

We rode up the dirt road toward town, Bett trotting along beside us.

"She'll turn back when we get to the end of the sheep meadow," said my father. "Her job is the sheep and she likes it."

Bett stopped at the sheep fence and watched us go off. Then she jumped through the fence to join the sheep.

A line of light appeared on the horizon as we rode.

Dawn.

My father patted Jack and began to sing softly.

"You're my buddy, my pal, my friend.
It will be that way until the end.
And wherever you go, I want you to know
You're my buddy, my pal, my friend."

"Willie Nelson," he said to me.

I knew.

His voice was strong and familiar. Sometimes my father sang to me at night when I was little—a different voice than my mother.

"You should sing with Mother sometime," I said to him as the sun came up and the prairie was filled with light.

"We do," he said.

"You do?! When?"

I was surprised and he smiled.

"At night after you're in bed."

"You do? Really?!"

"Really. You should hear your mother sing Willie Nelson."

"She sings Willie Nelson?!"

My father nodded. "And Johnny Cash. Roy Orbison too. Sometimes k.d. lang."

I stared at him, thinking for the first time about my mother and father's life together without Nate.

And without me.

"Look," said my father, pointing to Elmer Bean's cornfield.

Elmer had put one scarecrow out to keep away the crows. But now the field was filled with crows. It seemed like a hundred crows or more, and Elmer was putting up two more scarecrows. Fancy ones. One had a bright red jacket that I had seen Elmer wear. The other wore a fancy hat that Elmer's wife, Bella, wore on Sundays. It had a long ribbon that blew in the morning breeze.

I waved at Elmer and took out my notebook.

"This will help. It's a present from me to you," said my father.

He handed me a book. *An Exaltation of Larks.*

I opened it and found the names of groups of birds—finches and quail.

And crows!

"I never knew what a group of crows was called," I said.

I slid down off Molly and gave the reins to my father.

And I wrote.

My father and I rode home in the warm afternoon sun. We had dropped off my log of events to the sheriff's office.

"It was quite a list," said my father. "One small lost dog and a crying little girl looking for the small lost dog, a horse on his own on the road, a boy fallen off his bike—the parents called . . ."

"On my cell phone," I added.

"Don't forget Maude's flock of chickens running through town," I said.

"Lured home by a trail of grain," said my father. "That was smart of you to carry it."

We rode past Elmer Bean's scarecrows, colorful in the cornfield. Elmer had added bright spinning surprises on top of their heads.

"Only a few crows at the edges of the field," said my father. "But they'll be back. Crows are very smart and they have strong emotional connections with each other. They can recognize a face. And they can hatch plots."

"What kinds of plots?" I asked.

"Crow plots," said my father.

"How do you know that?" I asked.

"I've read about them. I'll tell you all I know."

We turned the corner by our sheep meadow and Bett came running to meet us.

At the barn we took off the saddles and washed the horses and wiped them down. We gave them water and grain, and opened the fence so they could go roll in the grasses of the field.

We walked into the kitchen. My father filled two glasses with cold water. He handed me one.

"Want to hear about the secret lives of crows?" he asked.

My mother walked into the kitchen, smiling at us. "How was your day?" she asked.

"It was great," I said.

"It was. I'm about to tell Sylvie all about the secret lives of crows," said my father.

My mother smiled at my father. "Your

father is fascinated by the secret lives of crows. And sheep, cows, and birds of the fields. And he's right. They all have secret lives of their own. One of the reasons I love living here."

I took a deep breath. "But don't you miss singing onstage?" I asked.

My mother stared at me for a moment.

"Only once in a while," she said. "But I'd miss you all the time if I went away to perform."

"Will you be glad to see James?"

"Of course. But he was my past. This is my present."

"And future," said my father.

I wanted to say, "But it is not exciting and glamorous. And we're just here on the farm."

But I couldn't say anything.

"Can I do anything for you before you hear about crows?" she asked.

"Yes!" I said suddenly. "You can sing a Willie Nelson song for me!"

My mother grinned. "He told you?" she said.

I nodded. "He knows all about your music. I just didn't know you know about his."

"But I do!" she said.

And she did.

She sang "I've Loved You All Over the World" with my father, and then they sang Johnny Cash, the two of them singing to each other like people falling in love in our kitchen.

My mother's voice was different. It matched my father's.

And they danced. Just danced. Like the day they met in the diner in Cheyenne.

I didn't learn about crows until later.

Not invited!

A murder of crows

Sly

Sleek

Eating the Bean field.

Come see the scarecrows!

Elmer in scarlet

Bella in her Sunday hat

Whirligigs on their heads

Amusing the crows as they

Keep on eating

And eating

And eating.

—Sylvie Bloom

*

Many Trails—

Of Millie Tinder's tears

Leading her to her lost best friend,

Ruby.

Furry
One black ear
And one white—
Licking Millie's tears away.

—Sylvie Bloom

*

A trail of grain,
Followed by
Maude's
Reckless
Running chickens,
Beaks on the ground
Until they are happily home again.

—Sylvie Bloom

• 4 •

Great Joy

Sheriff Ludolf came into the kitchen the next morning without knocking. He had a huge smile and handed me the morning newspaper.

"You're a great success, Sylvie!" he said loudly. "Here's your log."

He stopped suddenly to listen, the door open.

"What's Min singing? She sounds different! Nice, but different."

My mother did sound different. Her voice was smooth and strong.

"She's a mystery to me.
She's a mystery girl."

"I taught her that song. The sheep love it when Min sings Roy Orbison," my father said.

We were quiet in the kitchen.

Sheriff Ludolf sat down at the kitchen table. There were no sheep baas as there were usually.

"She'll still sing her own angel songs, won't she?" asked Sheriff Ludolf wistfully.

My father smiled at "angel songs."

"She's just enlarging her world a bit."

"I guess the truth of it is that Min can sing anything," Sheriff Ludolf said. "Everyone is reading your log and calling me, Sylvie. And there must be two dozen people at the Beans' cornfield, all looking at the Elmer and Bella scarecrows. They came from all over town when they read your invitation. So many people, the crows went somewhere else."

"They'll be back," said my father with a sly look.

The sheriff smiled. He beckoned to me. "All righty then. Our first day together in my car," he said.

Sheriff Ludolf and I walked out to his old black and white car with SHERIF stuck on the driver's side in black letters. The second *F* was gone.

He noticed my look.

"The last *F* fell off long ago. Not my fault. I stowed it somewhere," he said.

Beside us on the front seat was a dome light for the sheriff to put on top of his car, as a warning.

I pointed. "Do you ever use that?"

"Not often enough," he said. "Love it when I can. Got your cell phone?"

I held it up.

"All righty then!" said the sheriff.

"All righty then!" I repeated.

"Are you making fun of me?" he asked.

"I guess so, Sheriff Ludolf."

"You can drop the 'Sheriff.' And the 'Ludolf,'" he added.

"What should I call you?"

Sheriff Ludolf shook his head. "My mother called me Luddy Buddy."

We laughed together.

I thought for a moment.

"Could I call you Bud?" I asked.

He grinned. "Yes. That's what Ella calls me. Whoever can tell why mothers do what they do . . . naming me Rudolph Ludolf."

"Yes, mothers are a mystery," I said.

I sighed.

He started the car and looked sideways at me. He drove down the dirt road between the meadows.

"Surely not your mother," he said.

"She could be famous," I said softly.

He looked at me again and turned the corner until we came to a stop by the meadow fence.

He rolled down the window.

"She is famous to me," he said.

He was looking out the window, watching my mother feed the chickens. She was singing and the chickens were wildly eating.

"*The Magic Flute*," I said, sounding like my father.

"Sometimes when I drive by here and she's singing to the animals, I stop to listen."

"You do?"

He nodded and peered at me with a very serious face. "Your mother brings me great joy," he said.

My heart seemed to jump a little.

He turned and looked back across the field.

We didn't speak for a while.

And then I said something I hoped wouldn't insult him.

"You're pretty poetic for someone who can't spell," I said.

"I am?" he said with a small smile, still

watching my mother, hearing her voice float over the prairie grasses.

"Great joy," he repeated in a soft voice.

And we drove off, not speaking.

Buds

Bud and I drove for three days, getting to know each other. We crossed small country bridges over running streams, keeping watch over meadows, and driving on some dirt roads I'd never seen before. Surprises. Surprises. I was startled at the thought. I hadn't thought there would be surprises in my small town.

I liked driving with Bud. He talked some-times, telling me about the townspeople I didn't know. But he was quiet, too. He looked out his window and I looked out mine.

He turned up a hillside road.

"I don't come up here too often," he said. "Do you ride your horse up here ever?"

I shook my head. "Nope. Molly doesn't like going up hills. And she doesn't like coming down, either."

"Me neither," said Bud.

I looked to see if he was smiling and he was.

"Wait! Stop!" I said, sitting up straighter to look past Bud.

Bud stopped and picked up his binoculars.

"That's old Tinker Tibbs in his long underwear," said Bud.

I opened my door and got out.

"Behind him!" I yelled, running to the fence, climbing over.

The sheep in the meadow scattered.

"Make noise," I yelled at Bud. "An animal behind him is stalking him!"

I ran toward tall Tinker in his long underwear. Behind me Bud put the dome on the roof of the car and turned on his siren. The noise blasted over us all.

The sheep raced after each other, trying to hide from the loud noise.

I waved my arms at Tinker, but he walked on, not looking at me.

As I got closer Tinker looked over at me. Behind him a coyote, low to the ground, turned and ran off into the woods.

Bud turned off the siren and drove the car down a driveway.

"Hello," said Tinker, looking thoughtful. "Do I know you?"

I caught my breath. His eyes were the brightest blue.

"I'm Sylvie Bloom," I said. "A coyote was right behind you."

Tinker smiled a bit. "He often follows me," he said. "He pretends to stalk."

He looked more closely at me. "The Sylvie Bloom who writes the log?" he asked suddenly.

I nodded.

"You're good," he said.

We began walking toward Bud's car in the dirt driveway. There was a small cabin there, and a porch with chairs.

"Was that you making that noise?" Tinker asked.

"Sylvie was trying to save you from that coyote," said Bud.

"You mean Bernie?" asked Tinker. "I told Sylvie he often follows me. At night he sleeps on the porch. I found him as a pup."

Bud nodded.

"Come in," said Tinker, waving his arm as he walked up the steps.

Bud waved his arm, imitating Tinker, as we walked up steps and into Tinker's house.

There was a desk under a window, with papers, pens, and an old typewriter.

There were paintings on the walls.

There was a small, round dog bed next to the fireplace.

Tinker saw me looking at it. "That's where Bernie sleeps in the cold of winter," he said.

In the cold of winter?

I had never heard that phrase.

Bud looked at me. "Tinker's a reader," he said, as if that explained both the coyote bed and "in the cold of winter." "He observes life and sometimes writes about it in his journal."

"Like us," I said.

"Like you," said Bud and Tinker at the same time.

I walked to the wall where there was a pinned up written page.

> Birdsong ends at dusk
> Sun falls down into still night
> Barn owl wakes to hunt.

"That's a haiku," I said.

"It is," said Tinker happily. "I knew you were good!"

Back in the car, Bud said, "I don't think we should report anything about Tinker having a friendly coyote. Or that he was wandering a bit in his underwear."

I smiled. "No, but I think I'll write a haiku for him in my log."

Bud looked over at me. He sighed.

"What's a haiku?" he asked.

"You'll see. Just remember it is five-seven-five syllables."

Bud sighed again.

"Okay. Five-seven-five words."

"Syllables. It is an ancient Japanese form, like Tinker's haiku on the wall. It is very often about nature."

"Five-seven-five," said Bud again.

"You can ask Mrs. Ludolf about haiku. She knows everything," I said.

"I don't need her," said Bud, grinning. "I've got you. We are buds. That's short for buddies."

We are buds.

We drove down the hill and up and down roads. We passed the school where we found three young boys crouched over a pile of sticks.

"Fire," said Bud, coming to a stop.

Bud gave them a lecture and made them put out the fire before the wind spread it.

"Are we going to jail?" asked one boy, tears at the corners of his eyes.

"I don't put boys in jail," said Bud. "I tell their parents."

Tears fell down the boy's face.

"But not this time," said Bud. "I'm sure you will not build fires by yourselves again."

The boys nodded.

"Go on home now," said Bud kindly.

The boys ran off, not smiling or talking.

"All righty then," said Bud as we got in the car.

"The boys are more afraid of their parents than jail," I said to Bud as we drove away.

"My thought exactly," says Bud.

"All righty then," I said.

"All righty then," said Bud.

We passed Elmer's scarecrow field, where the crows were back.

"Just like your father said," said Bud.

"Yep. My father knows about crows. One day he's going to tell me all their secrets."

When we were on the road to my house, between two meadows, Bud stopped the car and rolled down his window.

My mother was in the meadow, feeding the sheep.

The sun was low in the sky.

The sheep had gathered around my mother.

She sang "*Casta diva*," slow and serene, her voice coming to us with the wind.

"She sang that once onstage in London," I said.

"And she sings it for us," said Bud.

I frowned at him and he caught me at it.

"Maybe one day you'll know why," he said.

"Know what?" I said crossly.

"It's your job to find out what," said Bud.

He tapped me on the arm and I couldn't be cross anymore.

It was the end of our day.

We saved little boys from jail and from their parents.

We saw the crows were back in Elmer's cornfield.

I met a reader who observed life.

Sheriff Ludolf and I were buds.

And I still didn't understand my mother.

Three Haikus

Sheep in the meadow
Blue-eyed man and a sweet friend
A good day of peace.

—Sylvie Bloom

*

Boys too young to say
Build a fire on windswept day
Sent home, ponder deeds.

—Sylvie Bloom

*

Wily crowd of crows
Back to plunder Elmer's corn
Maybe try sweet song?

—Sylvie Bloom

• 6 •

Haiku

Bud had gone off to a daylong sheriff's meeting.

I was surprised to see him arrive at our house with Mrs. Ludolf sitting in the passenger seat. It was early morning.

My mother was hanging sheets on the clothesline. My father came out of the barn with Nate.

Bud burst out of the car.

"Sylvie, would you believe that the

townspeople are singing at Elmer's corn-field? And there is a trumpet and a violin! Flutes to come. It seems you're not only reporting news, you're also making news."

"The crows will be back," said my father.

"Jack was a crow in his past life," said my mother with a grin.

Mrs. Ludolf gave me a hug, and I realized I'd missed her this summer.

"I miss you, too," she said as if she'd read my thoughts.

"Sylvie didn't say she missed you," said Bud.

"She was thinking it," said Mrs. Ludolf.

I nodded. "She knows."

Mrs. Ludolf did that. Reading the thoughts of her students.

"And all the parents of all the little

boys were calling me this morning to find out if their boy started the fire," Bud said. "Thankfully, all three gave themselves up."

He handed me the newspaper.

"And you wrote three haikus!" he said. "And believe it or not, Deputy Lula tried to write a parking ticket in haiku!"

I could believe that. I was in class with Lula's son Hank, who tried everything, both good and bad, and most times succeeded.

Mrs. Ludolf touched Bud's arm. "Show her," she said.

Bud reached in his pocket and took out a folded paper. He handed it to me.

It was a handwritten haiku.

"Bud! You wrote this?"

Bud shrugged. "I just did what you said."

I read it out loud.

"Birds fly down to hear
Sweet song for both sheep and man
She sings to bring joy."

Mrs. Ludolf beamed.

"This is about you," I said to my mother.

"It's about all of us," said Bud.

"It's about me!" said Nate suddenly, leaning against the wall.

My father reached out and smoothed his rumpled hair. I didn't say anything. I was afraid to speak about what I didn't understand. Except for one thing.

"Your haiku is better than mine," I said softly.

I handed it back to him.

Bud shook his head. "You keep it, Sylvie. I wrote it for you."

Blue Eyes, Yellow Eyes

I rode Molly today. I knew where I was going, and I left early, before it became too warm for Molly. There was no wind, and I could already feel the sun's heat.

We rode along the road, my mother singing, of course, music from *The Magic Flute* to the crazed chickens. I realized I was smiling, and I didn't know why. I put my hand in my pocket and found Bud's folded-up haiku there.

Molly liked being out on the road. She

tossed her head and began to trot. I turned her up the hill where she'd never been before. She didn't mind. We rode up the hill, past trees and clearings, hearing the songs of birds.

Molly tossed her head again. And then, past the field of four sheep, we came to Tinker's cabin. Tinker was on the porch reading a book.

I slid down off Molly and looped her reins over a low tree branch in the shade.

Tinker looked up and called to me. "Sylvie Bloom, the writer of haikus!"

Tinker walked down the steps and filled a pail with fresh water.

"Good morning, Tinker."

Tinker carried the pail over to Molly. She nosed his neck, making him smile.

"Molly's thanking you," I said.

"She's welcome," said Tinker.

His eyes were sharp and steady. And a blue I had no name for.

I sat on the top step and leaned against the porch post. Tinker sat in his chair, his long, lean legs stretched out.

"It was good the sheriff hired you. It was a wise choice."

"I like Bud. And I'm finding out a lot more about where I live. What's happening, sometimes surprising things. Surprising people. Like you."

I was looking out at the meadow, the sheep, and Molly in the shade.

"And," said Tinker in a hushed voice, "if you turn your head very slowly toward me, you'll see something else surprising. Slowly, remember."

I slowly turned my head and looked into

the very close, yellow eyes of Tinker's coyote.

I held my breath as Bernie stared at me for a long time. Then he sat. There were black spots like marbles in the middle of the yellow. He was so close.

"Ah, Bernie likes you," said Tinker. "I knew he would. You can talk, Sylvie. But I wouldn't touch him yet. That will come later, on your next visit."

Later, on my next visit?

I could feel my heart beating.

"Bernie," I said softly.

Bernie's ears went up. But he didn't move. He sat and watched.

I smiled.

"You're beautiful, Bernie."

He tilted his head as if considering this compliment.

The three of us sat on the porch for a long time, Bernie, Tinker, and I.

"My mother was a famous opera singer," I said suddenly, before I could stop myself.

Tinker did not look surprised.

He nodded. "I know that. I once heard her sing with James Grayson in London."

"Really?"

"Really," said Tinker. "I was a world traveler earlier in my life. Your mother has a stunningly beautiful voice."

I took a breath. "James Grayson is coming to the city to perform," I said.

"He has a beautiful voice too," said Tinker.

"Why do you think she doesn't sing onstage anymore?"

Tinker turned to look at me. "Perhaps it wasn't enough for her," he said.

"What more could there be?" I asked.

"You're sitting next to him," Tinker said softly. "For me," he added.

I turned to look into Bernie's yellow eyes.

"Bernie?" I whispered.

"Think about it, Sylvie," said Tinker. "Think about it."

Tinker kept looking at me.

Suddenly the sun came from behind a cloud. It was overhead, getting too hot for Molly. I got up to say good-bye.

Bernie never moved.

I walked down the steps, Tinker following me.

Before I left, I suddenly hugged Tinker.

"No one hugs me," he said, looking startled.

"I do," I said.

I got up on Molly.

"Come again," said Tinker.

"I will."

And as I rode off, Tinker called to me. "Think about it, Sylvie. You almost know."

For some reason, as I rode off, I felt tears at the edges of my eyes.

What was it I almost knew?

Molly and I went past the sheep meadow, past the woods, and down the hill again to the main road through town.

It was hot and I was sorry I'd waited so long to ride Molly home, even though Tinker had given her a pail of water.

We rode close to a car parked by the nature walk. The car windows were closed in the heat, except for the back windows, only open an inch.

I heard a noise. A dog was barking weakly

inside the car, watching as I came closer.

It was too hot for the dog, I could tell.

I slid off Molly and tried to open the doors, one by one, but the car was locked.

The dog nosed the open window and whined. I could see he was having trouble breathing.

I ran down the walking path and called loudly. "Whose car is this? There is a dog inside and it is too hot! Hey!"

I ran back up the path and I moved Molly to a tree where there was shade. I picked up a rock and tried to break a window. The rock bounced off the window.

The dog, a border collie, pawed at the window. I tried the rock again. The dog lay down on the backseat of the car, breathing hard.

I took out my cell phone. I dialed Bud's number.

He answered on the first ring.

I started crying.

"Bud. I need help! Dog locked in a hot car. I can't break the windows."

"Where?!"

"Nature walk!"

"I'm coming!"

Before he hung up I heard his siren through the phone.

I looked for a bigger rock. I found one too large to move, and my tears dropped on it as I tried to pry it loose.

I heard the sound of Bud's siren then, and I knew he was driving very fast. I could see the dome light turning.

He drove behind the car and slid to a stop.

He got out quickly, carrying a heavy iron bar. He looked very angry.

"Try to get the dog to the other window so I can break this one over here," he said.

I felt breathless. I spoke to the dog through the small space. "Hey, Pal, Bud's here."

The dog turned and slowly came over to my side. He was panting.

Bud crashed the driver's side window, and glass flew across the front seat. He reached in and unlocked the doors.

I opened my door and the dog licked my face and slowly jumped down to the ground. He lay down, and I sat on the ground next to him, stroking his soft fur.

Bud went to his car and hurried back with a bottle of water and a bowl.

"Here now." His voice was like a whisper.

He poured water into the bowl, and the dog got up and drank. And drank. He finished, and then he walked over to lean against Bud, who was sitting on the ground too.

"Hey, what are you doing?"

A man with a fishing rod stood by his car.

Bud stood very tall in his everyday clothes, jeans and a plain white shirt. The dog stayed next to him.

"I think the question is, what are you doing leaving a dog in a hot car?"

"Rascal is okay. Come, Rascal!"

The dog didn't move from Bud's side.

"And you broke my window!" the man yelled.

"The dog was not all right," I said suddenly. "He would have died in the heat. And that is against the law."

"You're just a kid," said the man.

"Let me introduce myself," said Bud. He held out his sheriff's badge. "I am Sheriff Ludolf and I broke your window to save the dog. May I see your driver's license please?"

The man pulled his wallet out of his pocket. He handed Bud his license.

Bud wrote down the information in his notebook.

"Thank you, Richard. And may I please see your fishing license?"

The man took a step backward.

"I don't . . . ," he began.

"Have one," finished Bud. "And you do not have a dog, either. We don't mistreat animals here."

"You can't do that," said the man.

"I can and I did. Move along now."

The man stared at Bud for a moment.

"But before you go I must confiscate your fishing equipment as well," said Bud. "It's the law."

Bud held out his hand and the man handed over his fishing rod.

He quickly opened the door, got in, and drove away.

"Do you think he knows he's sitting on broken glass?" I asked.

"Not yet," said Bud.

We heard a screeching of brakes.

"Now he knows," said Bud.

"Well, Pal, you're my dog now," said Bud. "Rascal is a dumb name for you. And Sylvie named you Pal."

Pal wagged his tail.

Bud looked at me. "Good job, Sylvie," he

said in his soft voice. "All righty then. Come on, Pal. It's Mrs. Ludolf's birthday. I can't wait to show her what I got her."

He opened the trunk and put the fishing rod inside. "Maybe I'll give Mrs. Ludolf the fishing rod as well."

Without a pause, Pal jumped in the backseat of Bud's car.

Bud smiled at me as Pal leaned over and licked his ear.

And as he drove off I could see two heads close together inside the car.

Bud and his dog.

"All righty then," I said to Molly as we headed home. She liked it when I talked to her.

I thought about Tinker and Bernie. I thought about Bud and Pal. I almost knew something. What was it? A breeze came up and blew my thoughts away. It was the end of my day.

> Find a yellow-eyed friend
> To look into your eyes.
> Find a wise blue-eyed friend
> To hug.
>
> —Sylvie Bloom

*

> Is there a word for today?
> A man breaks the glass of a hot
>   car,
> Saving a dog so they can care for
>   one another—
> The word is love.
>
> —Sylvie Bloom

In the night I wake from sleep with a sudden sharp memory of the thought a breeze had taken away—

Tinker had told me I almost knew.

The look of Bud finding his dog—

The look of Tinker with Bernie—family.

Was it family that was enough for my mother? Do I deserve this?

I turn on the light.

"Am I enough?"

I am surprised to hear myself say it aloud in the quiet dark.

I leave the light on. When I wake in the morning the light has been turned off by someone.

• 8 •

A Sweet Thing

Bud picked me up in the sheriff's car, with Pal sitting proudly in the backseat.

I saw that the last *F* had been stuck back onto the door. It now read SHERIFF.

I pointed to it as I walked to the car.

"Pal dug it out from under my driver's seat," Bud said. "He also found my favorite slippers under the bed and chewed on them."

I laughed. So did Bud.

"Pal loves you and your smell. You rescued him," Bud said.

I reached in the back window and gave Pal a hug.

"Maybe I'll grow up to be a sheriff," I said.

Bud smiled at me. "You will grow up to be an observer of life and a great writer," he said.

In the backseat there were two large bottles of water, a bowl, a bag of dog snacks, and a paper bag that I knew had doughnuts in it.

"Pal looks happy. How did Mrs. Ludolf like him as her birthday present?"

"Well, it was smart of me to buy her flowers and a bracelet as well," he said. "Except that I caught her slipping Pal food under the table as we ate. Remind her of that whenever she lectures your class about sneaky behavior."

"She has a soft heart," I said.

Bud started the car. "All righty then," he said briskly.

Pal made a noise and stuck his head between the two of us. When I turned my head, we were looking into each other's eyes

Eyes again.

"Pal's eyes are different. One eye is dark. One blue," I told Bud.

"I saw that."

"Bud?"

"Yes?"

"There's something you should know."

"What is that?"

I took a deep breath.

"The other day, before I found Pal in the car, I visited Tinker."

"And?"

"His coyote, Bernie, is his family. He lives with him. And I sat very close to him. And I looked into his eyes."

"I figured all that," said Bud. "Yellow eyes, right?"

"Yes."

"After your log I had three calls from teenagers asking about where they could find yellow-eyed girls."

I laughed.

"I'm trying to protect Tinker's privacy," said Bud. "I figure townspeople would be curious. And Tinker's a private person."

"Yellow eyes with a marble in the center," I said.

"I know."

"Do you know everything about everyone in town?" I asked.

"Yes."

"Do you know I want a doughnut now?"

"Yes," said Bud. "I know that."

We drove down the dirt road between the meadows.

Bud looked out the window, and I knew he was looking for my mother.

"She's singing to the chickens."

"*The Magic Flute?*"

"Of course. They are addicted to *The Magic Flute.*"

"Addicted chickens? Really?" Bud said, pretending to be alarmed.

He stopped the car to listen to her voice coming across the meadow.

Pal went over to the open window and heard too.

Pal sniffed. Then he lifted his head and began to howl.

I burst out laughing.

Way off I saw my mother straighten up and stop singing. She looked around.

Bud drove off quickly. He had a shocked look on his face.

We slowed down at the Beans' cornfield. There was a small chorus of singers today. The crows were still there.

Bud began to roll up Pal's window with a button on his door, in case Pal howled again.

It was too late.

Pal howled and a dark cloud of crows flew up and away.

"Could Pal be the solution, do you think?" Bud asked.

"Not according to my father. And you'd have to leave Pal with Elmer."

Bud shook his head. "He's my dog."

I knew he'd say that.

"Maybe you could leave Pal during the day and take him home at night?" I suggested.

"Nope. Pal likes riding in the sheriff's car."

I knew he'd say that, too.

We drove past the river and past sheep and cow meadows—all peaceful.

"Not any excitement today," I said, yawning.

"Wrong," said Bud, speeding up the car.

Up the road Mab Tilley was frantically waving her arms at Bud. Near the fence where she stood were a donkey and a goat.

Bud stopped the car and got out.

"Mab, what's wrong here?"

Mab burst into tears.

"I fed the donkey a large carrot and he's choking!"

The donkey was having trouble breathing, and his goat friend leaned against him. Mab fell into Bud's arms and nearly knocked him over. Mab was very large.

"Let's call your vet," said Bud.

"No," I called from the car, sliding over and getting out Bud's side. "This once happened to me when I fed Molly a carrot."

The donkey was wheezing now.

I reached over and stroked his long neck down firmly with one hand over and over, holding up his head with the other hand.

I did it again and again, and finally there was a sudden breath from the donkey.

"Oh dear, Sylvie," cried Mab, moving toward me.

I stayed with the donkey to keep Mab away. I worried she would knock me over.

And then the donkey put his head down next to my cheek and stayed there, breathing again. I reached out and patted him. It was a strange feeling, this warm donkey head so close.

Mab burst into tears again, but I kept hugging the donkey.

"I preferred the donkey to Mab," I admitted to Bud in the car.

Bud grinned. "I was nearly overcome by Mab myself. Nice work, Sylvie. I keep saying that to you," said Bud.

"My mother says we learn from our mistakes," I said. "Like the too-large carrot I fed to Molly once."

"Sylvie the philosopher," said Bud. "Then we don't have to make the same mistakes again, right?"

"Bud the philosopher," I said.

Pal barked from the backseat and put his face between us.

"Pal the philosopher!" Bud and I said at the same time, laughing our way home.

Will a barking dog scare the crows
   away?
Only for a moment's time,
And the crow cloud is back.
A dog cannot bark forever—
Though he may try.

                  —Sylvie Bloom

*

A sweet thing,
Saving Mab's donkey's life.
A sweet thing,
A donkey's head against
Your cheek
Saying thank you.

                    —Sylvie Bloom

• 9 •

Past and Present

I woke in the night shivering, and I pulled the quilt around me even though the night was warm. Outside my window were stars and a big moon. My father calls it a "strawberry moon" because some believe it is time for their fruit to ripen.

In the morning I had a headache and a sore throat. I could hear my mother in the shower doing her scales, up and down and up and down again—then arpeggios and trills.

I padded down the hallway and found Nate and my father sitting in there.

My father put his cool hand on my head. "You sick, Sylvie? You're very warm. No work for you today, I'm afraid."

"No, I'm not riding with Bud. He had to go to court."

"I hope there's no crime while he's gone," said Nate with a grin.

And then my mother began a new song.

I leaned my head back against the wall. My mother's performance posters would have called it "lyrical and moving."

"French," said Nate.

"'*Plaisir d'amour*,'" said my father, smiling. "'The Pleasure of Love.'"

He listened for a moment.

"That was the very first song your mother sang to me when we met."

He closed his eyes, and I thought about my parents before Nate and I arrived to clutter up their lives.

My father began singing so softly along with my mother, only Nate and I could hear.

"*My love loves me, a world of wonder I see. . . .*"

He looked at me with a shy look. "I can't sing like your mother."

"It doesn't matter," said Nate in his wise old man voice. And I had a sudden thought that everything Nate said I should be saying. I was older and I should be wiser.

My mother surprised us all by opening the door suddenly and catching us listening.

"I sang that for you," she said to my father.

My father smiled at her, standing there

wrapped in her bath towel, her hair still wet.

"Thank you, Min. But I've noticed the cows love it too."

"They do," said my mother. "I think they've been producing more milk. Have you noticed?"

My mother and father looked at each other. It was as if Nate and I were not there, listening to them, and watching them be romantic right in front of us.

Nate broke the silence. "Maybe you should hire yourself out to dairy farmers all around the town," he said.

My mother and father laughed a lot.

"I'm going back to bed," I said, grumpily leaving them laughing in the hallway.

• • •

I slept until afternoon, dreaming unwanted dreams of dancing and singing and people being romantic.

My mother came in with some soup and a thermometer.

She popped the thermometer under my tongue. She brushed back my hair to feel my forehead.

"You're over one hundred and two degrees, Sylvie. I'm calling Dr. Britt to see what he says."

"Oh no, I don't want to be sick," I said.

"I know. Let's see what Britty has to say."

I had to smile. My mother secretly called Dr. Britt "Pretty Britty" because he had a huge mop of black hair that he oiled.

"I'll get better without Pretty Britty. I will," I said.

My mother put her cool lips on my forehead for a moment, and then went away.

I woke to find Nate sitting on my bed, staring at me.

"Hi, Nate."

"You okay?"

"I'll be fine."

"The sheriff came by on his way home from Cheyenne and brought you something." Nate handed me a newspaper.

"It's marked," he said. "It has Mother's name in the article."

I read the article out loud.

"'James Grayson, acclaimed tenor, is coming to sing on June twenty-eighth in the Cheyenne Concert Hall. Mr. Grayson has performed in halls over Europe and in America, once singing with soprano

Melinda May, now Melinda Bloom, of Casper, Wyoming.'"

"James sent the tickets," said Nate.

"That's three days from now," I said. "I forgot it was coming up soon."

I had a strange feeling, between excitement and dread. Maybe it was because I was sick.

Maybe not.

"Maybe she'll want to go back to singing onstage," I said slowly.

I thought about that concert poster upstairs in the attic. The one of James Grayson and my mother onstage in London or Paris. Maybe Rome.

"Ha. Of course not! She'll see an old friend. From the past," said Nate, excited.

I looked at Nate. "How come you're so

different than I am?" I asked, not expecting an answer.

"You have preconceived notions," said Nate. "I don't."

I was so startled I could hardly talk.

"What do you know about preconceived notions? You're only eight."

"Soon to be nine. Mr. Hurley taught us in school that if we have preconceived notions, it often keeps us from the truth."

"The truth?"

"Maybe it is your truth and Mother's truth all mixed up in your head," said Nate.

I put the newspaper down on the bed and stared at Nate for so long, he finally said, "What?"

I could only shake my head because I had no words.

I stared more at Nate.

"Get the poster from the attic for me, Nate. Please?" I whispered.

And that was when I started coughing and had trouble breathing.

· 10 ·

Time to Say Goodbye

Dr. Britt and his shining hair had come and gone. I think another day went by. Then another. He left medicine, an inhaler to help me breathe, and a promise to come the next day.

"Pneumonia, Lamb Chop," he said to me, his oiled hair bouncing sunlight from the window across the walls of the room. "You have to stay in bed for at least three solid days. Maybe more."

I wondered what "three solid days" meant, until I remembered.

"I have a concert to go to tomorrow," I said, my voice sounding far away to me. I tried to sit up in bed but couldn't.

Dr. Britt shook his head. "Nope. Lots of water and lots of sleep," he told my mother and father.

Dr. Britt and my mother went downstairs.

My father sat on my bed. "While you are my captive I will at last tell you about the secret lives of crows," he said.

"But what about the concert?"

My father lifted his shoulders in a shrug.

"What?"

"Your mother and I will talk about it." There was a pause. "Someone will stay with you."

"You can stay with me," I said. "Mother and Nate can go."

My father was quiet. There was something he didn't want to say.

"All righty then," he said, imitating Bud. "The secret life of crows."

And he began to talk about crows—

"They feel grief.

"They gather when one dies.

"They have deep family ties.

"They know the faces of the humans they like."

My eyes closed, and then I heard—

"There was a small girl who fed the crows peanuts and food she had left over.

"In return the crows brought her small, shiny gifts of beads and other objects."

I heard everything he said—

Like a lullaby sung to a sleepy child.

And later I would remember it all.

In the evening, after Nate brought me soup, I heard my mother singing in the bathroom. It was far away from me, but I could hear her sing *"Plaisir d'amour."*

Then she began a song I remembered somehow. I heard her sing it to the cows once, calling them in for evening milking. *"Con te partirò."*

"It's a duet," she had said. "For two voices."

I turned on my light and leaned over to see the poster of my mother and James Grayson.

It was written there.

"Con te partirò"—"Time to Say Good-bye."

I got up very slowly, the first time I'd been

out of bed for two days—or three? I turned on my desk light, took out a blank sheet of paper, and wrote something for my log. I wrote for a while, then put the paper into my drawer to give to my father tomorrow morning. He'd give it to Bud.

I missed Bud and Pal.

Then I took out another piece of paper and wrote.

I wonder if it's my fault that Mother doesn't sing onstage anymore. The cows and sheep and chickens and goats keep her here.

Mostly Nate and I keep her here.

When I finished I was so tired. I lay down and pulled the quilt over me.

I don't remember falling asleep.

I never heard my mother and father come in to say good night.

Once I heard a rustle and looked up to see Nate sitting on my desk chair. I raised my head, but I was too tired and sick to talk to him.

• 11 •

The Secret Lives of Crows

I woke up early, feeling better. I wasn't coughing and my chest didn't feel so heavy.

When I walked to the window I saw our truck driving off between the two meadows. I couldn't see who drove the truck. It was too far away.

I looked at my calendar and suddenly the heavy feeling was back. It was concert day.

Mother and Nate were in the truck, and they wouldn't be back until evening.

The page I wrote in the night was not on my desk. I looked around but couldn't find it. The window had been open in the warm night. Maybe a breeze moved it.

The door behind me opened as I looked under my desk. My father.

"I saw them leave," I said, turning.

But it was my mother who stood there, a glass of juice for me in her hand.

"You?" is all I could say.

"Me," she said.

I sat on the bed and stared at her.

"Father and Nate left without you. That wasn't my plan," I said.

She smiled at me. "Maybe not your plan. But it was always mine."

She sat beside me on the bed and handed me the juice.

"Was Father angry?" I asked.

"It doesn't matter," she said.

"That sounds like something Nate would say," I said.

"I know," said my mother happily.

And instead of crying, which I felt like doing, we both laughed.

She handed me my pills.

"I stayed because I'm your mother and you are more important than a concert."

She stood up and looked out the window.

"Besides," she said with a faraway look, "I get letters from James all the time about where he's singing."

"You do?"

She nodded. "And the truth of it is every day I hear his tenor voice in my ear. He's always close by."

"Your past, Nate called it," I said. "And so did you."

It was quiet then.

Then mother put up the window a bit. "Here comes Bud!" she said. "You want a visitor?"

"I do," I said.

Mother smiled and I knew why. I sounded like Bud.

"All righty then," she said, making me laugh as she went downstairs to see Bud.

Bud and Pal arrived in my room together, Pal jumping up on my bed and licking my face.

"I've missed you!" I said. "Both of you."

"We've missed you, too," said Bud, sitting on my desk chair. "Crime is on the upswing."

"It is not," I said, laughing.

"Tinker asked how you are. He said that the log was no longer interesting."

"No, he didn't."

"No. But he was thinking it."

"You sound just like . . ."

"I know, I know," said Bud, waving his arms. "Mrs. Ludolf."

"I'll be back in a few days," I said.

"Good. The crows are still there."

"Bud?"

"Yes?"

"Reach into my desk drawer. I have an important log for you."

Bud opened the drawer and took out my paper. He read it.

"Oh, my," he said. "Oh, my. Your father told you this?"

"He did."

Bud stood up. "Come on, Pal. We have just enough time to get this in the afternoon paper."

Pal jumped off the bed and followed Bud to the door.

"Oh, my," said Bud again before he left.

I slept again.

I dreamed of crows.

The afternoon newspaper came, and my mother left it on my bed as I slept.

The Kindness of Crows

Someone I know taught me the
    secret lives of crows—
    and a child who fed them.
Crows left her shiny beads and stones
    and tiny bones—

It was a bargain—
Gifts of joy.

—Sylvie Bloom

It was dusk when I woke. I could hear my mother singing *"Plaisir d'amour"* to the cows as they hurried after her from the field to the barn.

Far off I could see the dust rise up from the tires of my father's truck, but the late light did not let me see him and my brother inside the truck.

I put on my jeans and slowly walked down the hallway and down the stairs to the kitchen. I looked out the door to see Nate climb out of the backseat. My father got out and waved to me.

Who was in the front seat? A hitchhiker?

We had them on our roads. Everyone picked up everyone they saw.

My mother sang in the barn. And a tall man got out of the front seat. I shaded my eyes against the late setting sun. Then I opened the door and went outside, the first time in days.

The man looked familiar. And then I knew. I knew because of the concert poster with his picture there.

James had come here.

He walked into the barn and we suddenly heard two voices singing. My mother and James Grayson.

My father came and put his arm around me. No words. Slowly we walked to the barn door and inside. Nate stood along the back wall.

And we all listened, and the cows stood staring, hearing two voices for the first time.

When they finished that song, they began, as I knew they would, *"Con te partirò."*

I looked up at my father and he bent down close so he could hear me.

"You did this?" I asked as softly as I could.

My father shook his head.

He pointed to Nate.

Nate? Nate did this?

No one spoke then. No cow mooed as they did most days.

The cows stood and listened.

We stood and listened.

Voices filled the barn.

We sat in the kitchen and the sun had set, though there was light outside. Bett had taken a liking to James. James sat with his long legs out, like Tinker, with his hand on Bett's head. His voice was musical, even when he spoke. I wanted to ask him if he could sing "You're my buddy, my pal, my friend" like Willie Nelson, but I didn't know him well enough.

James looked at me. "You are very much like your mother," he said. "You write about the things you care about, what you're getting to know, what you want to know, and what makes you afraid. You know more than you think you know."

I was quiet. Tinker had once said the same thing in his own way.

"Your mother is wiser than she knows too."

Nate sat down across from me.

"James didn't read the page you wrote

about Mother not singing onstage anymore being your fault," he said. "He didn't want to read anything that wasn't meant for him."

"Nate! You took that from my desk!" I said.

I could feel my cheeks blushing.

"Yes, and I told him what you wrote," said Nate. "I'm only eight, soon to be nine, remember, so I can do this."

This made Mother and Father and James laugh.

"Nate is wise like your father," said James. "Why would your mother want to sing onstage—travel away from you—when she has the largest audience in the world? The farm, the prairie, the sky, the birds, sheep and goats, pigs and cows. The moon and you?!"

"James was sometimes overly dramatic

onstage," said my mother with a sly smile.

"Say, I did some pretty swell dying scenes!" James said. "And I met my wife, Lily, by winking at her in the front row of the concert hall."

"In our love scene," Mother reminded him.

"I was reprimanded for that," he admitted. "And sent for acting lessons! But Lily and I married and now have six children."

"Six?" said Mother.

"Yes, a new boy named Reynard, which is French for . . ."

"Fox," said my father.

James smiled at my father. "So, is my intelligent lecture over?"

My mother laughed. "You did very well."

James leaned forward. "But am I right?" he asked, suddenly serious.

"You are very right," said my mother.

My father got up and poured more coffee into James's cup.

James tapped the newspaper with my crow log.

"Your mother brings gifts like the crows," he said softly.

I had a sudden memory of Bud in the car, telling me my mother brought him great joy.

"Life is simple. We silly humans try to make it complicated and confused. Confucius said that better. And your father is a hero for knowing it all along."

My mother leaned over and kissed my father on the cheek.

"One of the many reasons I married him," she said. "Plus he taught me the Texas

Two-Step. That was much harder than falling in love with Jack."

James peered at me. "Any questions?" he asked.

I thought.

"Were you and my mother boyfriend and girlfriend back then?" I asked.

James smiled at my mother. "Only onstage," he said softly. "We were in love onstage."

James tapped my hand. "The difference between your mother and me is that I love performing. Your mother loves singing. Wherever she is."

Nate smiled at me.

"Any other questions?" asked James.

"Yes," I said. "Can you sing Willie Nelson?"

My mother and father laughed.

"She asked me that once," said my mother.

"And what did you say?" asked James.

"I said yes!" said my mother.

And she and my father got up and began singing and dancing in the kitchen.

"You're my buddy, my pal, my friend,
It will be that way until the end.
And wherever you go, I want you to know
You're my buddy, my pal, my friend."

Suddenly the door swung open and Bud stood there. The room went quiet. Bud didn't seem to notice.

"Sylvie," said Bud. "After they read your log, the townspeople are lining the sides of Elmer's cornfield with bits of bread and peanuts. Even cashews for the crows! Pancakes, too. And several croissants were seen!"

Bud looked at James.

"I'm Bud, the sheriff," he said. "Am I to assume you'll be singing to the cows and sheep tomorrow morning?"

"I will," said James. "And the pigs."

"Not *The Magic Flute* to the chickens," said Bud.

"Never!" said James, making my mother laugh.

James leaned down to whisper in my ear. "I think I'd like to live here forever."

I looked at him and surprised myself.

"Me too," I said.

Today two voices ride
The wind over meadows—
Today the crows eat sweet cakes—

And leave seven shiny beads,

Leaving the corn to Elmer.

A deal is made.

Life is simple.

Just dance.

—Sylvie Bloom